Don't you know You are Beautiful Just the Way You Are!

G.A Sealy

First Edition
Printed in China
Published in 2017

978-0-9965978-2-1 Large Print Paperback

978-0-9965978-3-8 Large Print Hardcover

Books may be purchased by contacting the publisher and author at dawitpublishing@gmail.com or visit www.dawitpublishing.com

This book is dedicated
to my daughter Dasia,
and my niece Abby
who were the inspiration
for this book.

Acknowledgements

I would like to thank
my family and friends
for all their support,
and Dr. Marcus Broadhead
who helped me edit my
book in its early stages.

FASHION
FASHION
FASHION
FASHION

In a sad voice Destiny said,
"Mommy I don't like the way I look.
I want to look like the girls in my
class, and the models in the book."

Mommy replied,
"Sweetheart, why would you say such a thing my little shining star? Don't you know you are beautiful just the way you are?"

Destiny said
"I don't like my flat round nose.
I wish it was pointy and straight
like my friend Rose."

Mommy gently held Destiny's face.
"Don't be silly. You have such a
cute button nose that is perfectly
suited for your beautiful face.
If you had any other nose it
would be simply out of place,
my little shining star.
Don't you know you are beautiful
just the way you are?"

Destiny pointed to the t.v.
as she sighed,
"I wish I looked like that girl
Amber from my favorite show."

Mommy hugged and kissed
Destiny.
"You are more beautiful
than you even know.
You are smart, and funny and
you are as sweet as honey."

"You are kind and caring,
compassionate, and sharing.
Your beauty starts from within,
and flows far deeper than
your face, hair or skin.
My little shining star,
Don't you know you are beautiful
just the way you are?"

Destiny then touched her hair.
"I don't like my thick hair. I wish
it was long straight and flowing,
like my friend Clare's."

"Destiny, you have a gorgeous head of hair! Your hair is so strong and healthy, and can be styled in so many ways."

"You can wear your hair in locks,
buns, as well as braids.
Your thick beautiful hair is a blessing,
my little shining star.
Don't you know you are beautiful
just the way you are?"

"Mommy what you
are saying maybe true,
But my lips are too big, and
I wish they were smaller too."

FASHION
SURGERY

Mommy said "Why in the
world would you want to?
Don't you know that some
women in magazines would love
to have lips just like you?"

So don't look in those
magazines for your image of
beauty because God created
you perfect my little cutie.

From your curly hair,
to your exquisite round nose

From your caramel skin
that in the sun starts to glow

From your vibrant brown
eyes and full pink lips

From your beautiful brown
arms and legs, attached to
your beautiful brown hips

Look at your aunties, grandmas,
and your cousins
Destiny you are surrounded by
beautiful women by the dozens!

Destiny smiled.
"Mommy that's true,
because you are beautiful,
so I must be beautiful, because
I look just like You."

I AM BEAUTIFUL
INSIDE AND OUT.

You are so beautiful
it makes me want to shout!

I am beautiful even though
I am not a t.v. star.

Mommy embraced Destiny.
"My little shining star,
You are beautiful
just the way you are."

G.A. Sealy is an author and owner of DaWit Publishing LLC. He currently lives in Georgia with his family, and in his spare time loves to travel abroad to experience different cultures. Look out for other books in his I Love Me Series, and his Young Scientist Series of books. For more information about the author, or any of his books, please contact dawitpublishing@gmail.com or go to www.dawitpublishing.com

Made in the USA
Monee, IL
26 July 2020

37056780R00033